I0727237

LUCKY
Shenanigans

LUCKY SHENANIGANS

PEPPER MCGRAW

CONTENTS

Cover and Inside Images from Dreamtime:
Girl Leprechaun on Shamrock © Baken
Shamrock Ornamental © Ilyach
Designs for St. Patrick's Day © Dip2000
Magic Clover Background © Stekloduv
Shamrock Background © Kirsty Pargeter
Background with Shamrock © Naddiya
Heart shamrock © Anker
Background with clover © Nelli Valova

ISBN 978-1-951247-29-4

Edited by J.L. Troughton
PMG Publishing

"ALL YOU HAVE to do is convince the dragons," Lucky's mother said. "Should be easy enough."

Lucky groaned. "*Easy?* Have you *seen* the dragons? They're huge! And unlikely to be open-minded."

"Well, then try the fairies first," her father advised.

"The fairies?" Lucky exclaimed. "Are you insane? What if I get caught? They're vengeful and mean!"

"You're a leprechaun," her brother, Charming said. "We don't get caught!"

"Besides, we leprechauns have always gotten along with the fairies," her mother said.

"Yes," Lucky said dryly. "And that's why we've been banned from the fairy mall for almost three hundred years."

"Eh, semantics." Her mother waved a hand in the air as if to dismiss even the thought of their banishment, though it was the reason for this whole mission in the first place.

"The fairies were just making a point," her father said. "I'm sure they've forgiven us by now."

Yes, because fairies were known for being so forgiving.

"It really can't be that difficult, Lucky," her mother said. "The other leprechauns have already paved the way. All you have to do is show up, get the attention of the dragons and the fairies by tapping into your trickster instincts and everything will turn out just fine."

"My trickster instincts won't save me if the fairies catch me wreaking havoc."

"I told you," Charming said. "Leprechauns don't get caught."

"And certainly not by fairies or dragons," her mother said. "We're far superior to pretty much any other being of the realms. Besides, we're not just your *average* leprechauns. We're royalty!"

Lucky grimaced. Again with the royalty nonsense. "We haven't been royals in a century, Mother. No one uses our titles anymore. We *are* average leprechauns now."

"Don't be ridiculous. You're *still* a princess and nothing will ever change that reality, my dear. Now chin up and go trick those dragons and fairies into giving us everything we've ever wanted!"

"*Everything?*" Lucky exclaimed incredulously.

"Oh, just go already!"

Lucky smirked, flicked the space in front of her and zipped into the tiny fold she created there. A quick flick behind her and the fold slammed shut right in her brother's face.

She grinned as his angry shout followed her into the next realm.

Earth.

Why the fairies and dragons had chosen *this* realm, Lucky had no idea.

Well, okay, it probably had something to do with their mates.

In fact, it was because of these mates the leprechaun mission was a go in the first place. As it turned out, one of the dragons was mated to the manager of a Shenanigans bar. Even better, this particular bar was located inside a *Hotel* Shenanigans managed by the mate of a *fairy*.

Two incredibly lucky developments for the leprechauns since all Shenanigans were neutral territories, which meant the leprechauns finally had access to not just the dragons, but the fairies themselves.

This, of course, meant they now had a tiny pocket of opportunity to potentially reverse their banishment.

Or not.

Lucky was certain this mission the Leprechaun Nation had united to embark upon was doomed for failure. Still, despite her dire predictions and her enjoyment of torturing her family with her protests, Lucky was very much looking forward to this adventure.

She was absolutely certain things were going to get out of hand fast. Which in her world, equaled a whole lot of *fun*!

o you have any idea how unusual it is to see one leprechaun, let alone several at a time?" Markos demanded.

Cassie rolled her eyes. "Um, yes, I do have a bit of an inkling."

"You do?"

Cassie had no idea why Markos was so surprised to hear this. She ran a Shenanigans, for heaven's sake. "You know I worked at a variety of Shenanigans before settling here. And in all those Shenanigans, not once did I meet a leprechaun."

Markos huffed. "Those were earth-bound Shenanigans and they weren't even in Ireland. Of course, you weren't going to see any leprechauns there. That's not the point."

"He's right," Zee said.

"Then what is the point?" Ashlynn asked. "Because I'm as confused as Cassie."

"The point is it's rare to see a leprechaun at all, and never in groups."

"Exactly." Markos pointed to his brother. "They're up to something."

"Okay, did you ever stop to think that it might be connected to the fact that *this* Shenanigans is inside a *hotel* Shenanigans where all the realms converge?" Cassie asked.

"Plus it's a bar," Ashlynn said. "Don't leprechauns love to drink?"

Zee groaned. "You just don't get it."

"You're right. I don't," Ashlynn said.

"What does it matter anyway?" Cassie asked.

Zee and Markos looked at each, then back at their mates, incredulous looks on their faces.

"What?" Cassie exclaimed. Before they could respond, she held up a finger. "Hold that thought." She headed for the opposite end of the bar where she took a couple orders, handed out drinks, then headed back to her mate and their friends. "Okay, explain."

"Leprechauns," Zee said, "visiting *this* bar."

When Cassie just shook her head at him and Ashlynn cast him a confused look, he repeated, "*This* Shenanigans."

"Right. Where all the realms converge," Cassie said again.

"Cassie," Markos sighed. "*This* Shenanigans. A known dragon hangout."

Ashlynn and Cassie looked at each other, then back at their mates.

"So what?" Ashlynn asked. "Are they supposed to

be scared of you or something?"

Cassie grinned. "Tell me you guys don't eat the leprechauns."

"What a horrible development that would be," Ashlynn said with a giggle.

"Is that a joke?" Markos demanded, a look of horror and disgust on his face.

"Of course, it was, darling." Cassie bit her lip to keep from laughing out loud.

He stared at her suspiciously.

"We're getting off track," Zee said. "Think about it a minute."

"I *am* thinking about it," Ashlynn said. "Dragons and leprechauns. Still don't get it."

Cassie shrugged. "I'm with Ashlynn on this one."

"Okay, let's try this," Zee said. "What do you know about leprechauns?"

"They wear green," Ashlynn said.

"They're probably Irish or maybe fairies," Cassie said.

"Or Irish fairies," the women said together, then grinned at each other and exclaimed, "Jinx!"

Markos stared at them a moment, then shook his head in exasperation. "What else?"

"Shoes," Ashlynn said.

"Shoes?" Cassie asked.

"They have those weird, curved shoes. And maybe they like to make them? Or eat them? I can't remember."

Zee let out a growl.

Ashlynn scowled at him. "Hey, don't growl at me!"

"Seriously? That's all you two know about leprechauns?" Markos demanded.

"Oh!" Cassie exclaimed. "Rainbows!"

"Oooh, and pots of —" Ashlynn broke off, stared at Cassie and they both said at once, "Ohhh."

"Tell me you're not planning to steal the leprechauns' gold." Cassie said.

Markos shrugged. "Hey. It's their responsibility to make sure their hordes are safe."

"Yeah," Zee agreed. "Especially from dragons."

"I don't think leprechauns have hordes," Cassie said.

"Probably because dragons keep stealing them." Markos grinned.

"Stealing is wrong!" Ashlynn admonished him.

"Plus they're leprechauns. They're like tiny, baby fairies. And you're dragons! It's a little unfair, don't you think?" Cassie asked.

"Unfair?" Zee and Markos exclaimed. They looked at each other, then burst into laughter.

"What?" Ashlynn and Cassie demanded together.

"That's hilarious," Zee said.

Markos nodded. "Next thing you know they'll be telling us not to be mean to the poor, innocent leprechauns."

Zee let out a snort of laughter.

"You know." A new voice intruded on their conversation. "Speaking from experience here: it's never a good idea to mess with the leprechauns *or* their pots of gold."

"Darren!" Cassie exclaimed, then darted around the bar and flung herself into her brother's arms.

Though Darren had seen Cassie several months before when he'd maneuvered the Council into visiting to make sure she was safe and happy, it had been an extremely short visit—their first one in years, in fact—and had been awkward at best. So when Cassie lit up at seeing him again and threw herself into his arms, for one long moment, he froze in surprise.

Then, muscle memory kicked in and his arms closed tight around her and for one too-short moment in time, Cassie was once more his baby sister and he was the center of her world.

"Ah, Cassie, it's good to see you, love."

She pulled back. "I've missed you so much, Darren. I'm so happy you're here and *early*!"

He smiled at her. "I thought it'd be nice to spend some time with my sister before her mating ceremony. You don't mind, I hope."

Cassie beamed at him. "Are you kidding? This is the best surprise ever!"

Darren chuckled. "I'm happy to hear it. So what's all this about leprechauns?"

Cassie waved a hand in the air. "The better question is what's with the dragons?" She turned and stared at her mate. "They're all wound up because we've had leprechauns drinking in the bar every night for the past month."

"The same leprechauns?" Darren asked. If it was the same group, that would probably be—

"Not at all," Markos said, motioning Darren to grab a bar stool and join them. "Different leprechauns every night."

"Okay, that's not true," Cassie said as she walked back around the bar. "They like to mix it up, so it's not the same group every night, but it is the same leprechauns week after week."

"How many are we talking about?" Darren asked.

"Hundreds," Zee grumbled.

"Are you serious?" Darren asked.

"He's exaggerating!" Ashlynn giggled. "It's probably no more than fifty total."

"*Fifty* leprechauns?" Darren exclaimed incredulously. "In one place at the same time?"

"See? That's what we're talking about!" Zee exclaimed.

"It's not fifty leprechauns!" Cassie said. "Stop exaggerating. It's maybe five or six a night. And okay, maybe over the course of a week it could be thirty or forty different leprechauns, but still."

"Six in one night?" Darren said. "That's not good."

"I told you, Cassie!" Markos exclaimed. "Even your brother agrees."

"They're definitely up to something," Darren said.

"Exactly!" Zee said. "And that's why we're going to steal their pot of gold. Serves them right."

"You don't even know what they're up to," Ashlynn said. "Could be something completely innocent."

Darren shook his head. "Not possible. Leprechauns aren't innocent by any stretch of the imagination."

"And how would you know that?" Cassie asked.

"Remember the Dublin con?"

"The one in Ireland that didn't go so well?"

That was one way of putting it. "Yes. The only con I ever led that *failed*."

She nodded. "I remember."

"Well, I blame that failure on the leprechauns."

Cassie grinned. "Are you serious right now?"

"Completely. We didn't know it at the time, but we were targeting a family the leprechauns claimed as their own. Some weird connection from back in the 1300s. Ridiculous, really. But the leprechauns were quite put out."

"How did they figure out you were chameleons?"

"Oh, they didn't. They figured we were a rival band of leprechauns."

"Oh, dear."

"Yep. All I have to say is, it's a really good idea to avoid crossing the wee folk."

"Isn't that the con where Jackson came back with a broken leg?"

Darren grinned at the memory. "Yep. Like I said. Best not to cross them. Honestly, though, I rather enjoyed that development. Couldn't have happened to a nicer guy."

Cassie giggled. "You're terrible. Jackson's not that bad."

Markos let out a growl and Darren smirked. If there was one chameleon Darren knew that Markos hated, it was Jackson.

"Markos, don't be mean. Jackson's just… gullible."

Well, that was one word for it. The chameleon had been determined to mate with Cassie all because the Council had claimed they were destined to do so. The man never even questioned why if they were mates, he didn't miss Cassie when she was gone.

Actually, gullible was probably the right word for it It was why the Council wanted him to mate with Cassie in the first place. He was too gullible to be a successful chameleon and Cassie had too much of a conscience. So the Council figured they'd pair the two of them together and minimize the damage so to speak.

Luckily for Cassie, she'd found her mate among the dragons.

Too bad Jackson hadn't found his.

If one of his chameleons had to leave the Coalition, Darren would have preferred it be Jackson and not his sister. But looking at Cassie now, as she leaned across the bar to kiss the grumpiness from her mate's expression, Darren knew this was the best possible result for her. He missed her, and always would, but that was okay as long as she was happy, which was all he'd ever wanted for his baby sister.

"Well, there aren't any leprechauns in here right now, so I guess maybe you were wrong about them being up to something, Zee," Ashlynn said.

That was when a bunch of leprechauns started popping into the bar out of thin air, one after the other. And they didn't stop at five or six.

Zee raised an eyebrow. "You were saying?"

2

MISCHIEF LEAPT TO his feet the instant Lucky appeared. "It's about time."

"Hurray!" The rest of the leprechauns cheered. "We get to go to earth now. We get to go to earth now!"

"Okay, calm down." Lucky grinned at her fellow leprechauns. They got so excited about the silliest of things. "Haven't you been to earth every night for the past several weeks?"

"Well, sure, but now you're here and the fun can really begin!" Peppy exclaimed.

Lucky giggled. "Also, aren't we already on earth?"

"Well, sure, but no one can see us, so it doesn't really count," Nosy said. "Look!" He pointed at the shimmering barrier that gave them the ability to see anything they needed to see without anyone knowing they were there.

Lucky stepped forward to stare across the barrier. "Is that Shenanigans?"

"It sure is. Look, there are already a couple dragons sitting at the bar with a phoenix, but don't be fooled by the bartender. She's not a leprechaun," Brainy said.

"She's tricky," Loopy agreed. "We thought she was one of us for a while, and we were quite impressed."

"Yes," Nosy agreed. "We couldn't believe we'd gotten a leprechaun undercover at a Shenanigans."

"But then we heard one of the dragons call her Cassie," Mischief said sadly, "and that's when we knew."

"Knew what?"

"That she's the chameleon."

"Ah, the mate of one of the dragons." The woman was quite infamous throughout the realms. A chameleon who had managed to hide her true nature from the dragons themselves. Only her mate could see her true nature. The rest of the dragons, all of them, had believed she was one of them. A most unusual, most talented chameleon.

Oh, the tricks they could play with a chameleon such as she on their team.

At that moment, Charming popped in beside Lucky and whacked her on the back of her head.

"Hey!" Lucky smoothed her hair down and scowled at her brother.

"Don't hey me. It took me a while to track you down. I can't believe you left me like that."

Lucky rolled her eyes. Seriously. Her brother could get lost walking from one end of a four-foot tunnel to another.

"Prince Charming!" The rest of the leprechauns cheered, then immediately burst into laughter.

Ugh. Lucky almost gave herself an aneurysm, she rolled her eyes so hard. The Leprechaun Nation had ditched the titles more than a century before, but that didn't stop the leprechauns from using them around Charming.

They thought it was hilarious, as was quite evident from the way they were all chortling and muttering, "Prince Charming," over and over again.

"Okay, that's enough," Lucky snapped. "Let's get this over with, shall we?" She started to step forward, but Charming caught her by the arm and hauled her back from the shimmering veil.

"Oh no, sister. We're doing this in style. Mischief, would you start us off please?"

Mischief beamed in joy, straightened his green vest, puffed out his chest and solemnly strode his way through the barrier.

As the leprechauns arrived, they swiveled to face each other, creating a line of leprechauns down the middle of the bar and then right in front of the doors a pair of leprechauns appeared.

One of the leprechauns was unlike any Darren had ever seen before.

"Is that—?" Markos began

"A lady leprechaun," Zee said. "I thought they were just a myth."

"Princess Lucky," one of the leprechauns shouted.

Darren could swear he saw the woman roll her eyes at that proclamation.

Surely not.

"And Prince Charming," another leprechaun bellowed.

This time, Darren was positive the lady rolled her eyes. He also thought she sneered a bit.

That was when the leprechauns began to chortle and giggle.

Though not, Darren noticed, the Princess Lucky or Prince Charming.

Instead, arm in arm, the two progressed solemnly down the line of snickering leprechauns, nodding regally to each one as they passed him by.

"I thought all the leprechauns were men," Ashlynn said.

"That's what I heard," Cassie said. "No females allowed."

Darren was too busy staring at the only female leprechaun he'd ever seen to respond.

She was exquisite!

Dressed all in green with a matching hat set at a jaunty angle atop a riot of red curls, she had a mischievous grin on her face and her eyes danced with delight.

Delight that is, until she heard Markos say rather loudly, "What kind of trickery is this? There's no such thing as a lady leprechaun!"

Her smile disappeared, her eyes narrowed and she said in a rather exasperated voice, "Tell me that ridiculous rumor isn't still going around."

"It's just a rumor?" Ashlynn asked.

"Of course, it is. How exactly do you think leprechauns are born if there aren't any females?"

Markos shrugged. "Eh, I just figured they were always one gender."

"I never really thought about it," Zee said.

"Asexual reproduction?" Ashlynn offered.

Princess Lucky rolled her eyes. "Whatever. Lady leprechauns *do* exist, thank you very much."

"We just don't let them out very often," Prince Charming said, slinging an arm around her shoulders.

Darren's eyes narrowed, annoyed at the thought that these two might be a couple. He couldn't possibly be that unlucky, could he?

"Ugh. Get off me." Princess Lucky shoved Charming away from her. "More like we're better at hiding than our idiot male relatives."

"Hey!"

Darren grinned. This was promising. "So you're not—"

"We're not what?" The princess asked a split second before her eyes widened. "Oh, dear goddess of tricksters, no. He's my idiot brother."

"Hey!"

The leprechauns, who had all dispersed to tables around the room, snickered.

The princess smiled at Darren. "You want to grab a table?"

Darren leapt from his seat. "Definitely." He couldn't believe of all the paranormals in the room, she had singled him out. He led her to a table in a shadowed corner of the bar, thanking his lucky stars for his sister's mating.

Cassie grinned as she watched her brother lead the princess to a table. "I can't believe it," she whispered.

"What?" Ashlynn asked.

"Remember when I asked Val for help? I think it worked."

Ashlynn swung around and stared at Darren and the princess as they settled at a table in the corner. "Wow. That was really fast."

"No kidding!"

"Well, fine," Charming shouted, making Cassie jump. He was glaring in his sister's direction. "I'll be over here. Drinking. Alone."

At that moment, one of the leprechauns shouted across the room, "Charming, drinks!"

Charming lit up and swung toward Cassie. "We need—" He glanced over his shoulder and took in the number of leprechauns in the room. "We'll say ten bottles, no, better make that twenty, of Tricky Charms."

Tricky Charms was one of those potentially dangerous drinks every waitress and bartender had to learn about in order to work at a Shenanigans, but Cassie hadn't had a chance to serve it until very recently when leprechauns started showing up night after night.

Now she had it delivered every week, along with all the other alcohols being consumed on a regular basis. She kept having to increase her order though because the leprechauns could put away some serious amounts of alcohol.

She'd also learned it was much easier to just leave the bottles in their boxes.

She stepped to the side of the bar and grabbed one of the boxes stacked against the wall there. She carried it back and set it on the bar. "There's ten bottles in there. I'll get you another box and start you a tab."

Charming grinned, grabbed the box and

wandered off, distributing the bottles as he went. A few moments later, he returned for the second box, winked at Cassie and wandered away again.

"Don't you want any glasses?" Cassie called after him.

He just laughed and kept walking.

Cassie shook her head. "They never want glasses. I keep asking, but they apparently prefer drinking straight from the bottle."

"Leprechauns," Markos said, disgust in his voice. "There's no explaining them."

"I'm curious about Tricky Charms," Ashlynn said. "Have you tried it, Cassie?"

"No way. I've heard the stories. You can't have worked at a Shenanigans and not have heard them."

"What stories?" Kitty showed up, Logan at her side, and hopped onto a bar stool.

"Hey, guys!" Ashlynn exclaimed. "I was just about to try the leprechaun drink, Tricky Charms. Want to join me?"

"I'm not sure that's a good idea," Zee said. "After all, it's a drink made by tricksters."

"Oh, don't be ridiculous," Ashlynn said.

"I have to agree with Zee on this one," Logan said.

"You cannot trust the leprechauns," Markos said.

"*They're* drinking it and nothing's happened to *them*," Kitty said.

"Exactly," Ashlynn said. "Who's joining us?"

"Not I," Markos said.

"Nor me," Zee said.

"I'm out," Logan said.

"I guess it's just two Tricky Charms, for the only ones courageous enough to try it," Ashlynn said.

"Will you join us, Cassie?" Kitty asked.

"Not a chance." Cassie grabbed two wine glasses and poured their drinks. As the liquid sloshed into the first glass, a tiny charm appeared around its stem. A moment later, the same thing happened with the second glass.

"Look!" Kitty exclaimed, reaching for her glass. "It's a tiny shamrock!"

"Mine too," Ashlynn said, lifting her glass to stare at the charm.

Cassie rolled her eyes. "Yes, well, feel free to keep the charm. Just know that Shenanigans is not responsible in any way for those tricky charms. You should direct all complaints to the Leprechaun Nation."

Cassie had been required to memorize that warning when hired at her very first Shenanigans years before, yet even though this was the first time she'd ever had to deliver it, the words flowed off her tongue as if no time had passed at all.

To be honest, she wasn't exactly thrilled that the first people she had to deliver the warning to were friends of hers, especially since she had no idea what the repercussions might be, and neither of her friends seemed be taking it seriously.

Ashlynn was already unhooking the charm from around the stem of her glass and slipping it onto the corded necklace she wore while Kitty was adding her charm to a bracelet.

"I'm so glad I wore my charm bracelet today. It fits perfectly right here. See?" Kitty lifted her arm and shook it gently so that all the charms jingled merrily. "The shamrock's so cute!"

Cassie wanted to agree, but truthfully, she was afraid. And she could tell by the looks on the dragons' and fairy's faces that they were worried too.

3

LUCKY COULDN'T TAKE her eyes off the gorgeous man seated at the bar. He had dark skin and gorgeous brown eyes she could drown in.

She was supposed to be mingling with the dragons and the fairies, but it wouldn't hurt to add chameleons to that list. Right?

It was interesting that she knew he was a chameleon. The bartender, she would have thought was a leprechaun if her friends hadn't warned her otherwise.

This man, though, must not be a very good chameleon if Lucky could see through his disguise to his true self so quickly.

She couldn't resist inviting him to a private table, in the hopes of getting to know him better.

As he led her away from the bar, she could hear her brother being an idiot in the background, but she just ignored him. Something she was very good at doing.

"So you're a princess," the chameleon said as he pulled out a chair for her—so charming—then settled in the one across from her.

"No," Lucky said. "The leprechauns sometimes cling to tradition, plus it makes them laugh every time they say 'Prince Charming,' and leprechauns do love their laughter."

The chameleon grinned. "I noticed. I'm Darren Prescott, by the way."

What a wonderful name. "And I'm Lucky, though not really. Or at least no luckier than any other leprechaun."

"And are leprechauns naturally lucky?"

Lucky shrugged. "Your guess is as good as mine. Is it lucky that we're so good at tricks or is it natural talent? I mean, we *are* leprechauns."

Darren laughed. "So, Lucky, tell me all about yourself."

That was how Lucky ended up spending her first

evening at the Shenanigans in the earth realm flirting with a chameleon rather than making friends with the dragons and fairies.

"That's it," Markos said, slamming down his drink. "I'm going in."

"Wait, what?" Cassie turned from where she was serving a couple trolls to stare at her mate.

"Those leprechauns are up to something and I'm going to figure out what it is."

"I'll join you," Zee said.

Logan grinned, leaned over and kissed Kitty's cheek. "I should probably go with them. It's highly likely they'll offend the leprechauns and then where will we be?"

Kitty giggled. "Well, have fun, darling."

"You two need to be nice to those leprechauns," Ashlynn admonished as her mate downed the last of his drink and hopped off his stool.

Zee gave her an innocent look. "What are you talking about? We'd never hurt the wee folk."

"Never," Markos agreed. "It's their gold they

should be worried about." With that, the three men sauntered off, crossing the bar to where Charming and a group of rowdy leprechauns were laughing hysterically.

Cassie shook her head. "This cannot be good."

*L*ogan followed the dragon brothers, thinking they probably had no plan and were headed for disaster.

Zee must have thought the same because at that moment he muttered to Markos, "So, what's the plan?"

"Get them drunk, then follow them back to their gold."

That was their plan? "You two are delusional." Logan darted in front of them and faced the dragons, forcing them to halt. "You do realize leprechauns are master tricksters. They'll see you coming a mile away. Not to mention, they may get drunk—all the time, mind you—but they never lose their wits. And frankly, attempting to follow a leprechaun is an exercise in futility."

"You've never seen us in action," Zee said.

"Exactly!" Markos agreed. "Just watch and learn, fairy. Watch and learn."

The dragons diverged, moving around Logan and making a beeline for the closest table of leprechauns.

Logan closed his eyes, shook his head, then spun and followed the idiots to their doom.

As far as Markos was concerned, he and Zee were quite smart in their approach. They offered to buy the leprechauns a drink and were instantly invited to join them. Their mistake was offering to share a bottle of Dragon Flame, which meant in order to be polite, they had to accept the offer of Tricky Charms in return.

Markos was rather relieved when Charming produced a couple glasses for the dragons, which was very nice of him. Markos had worried for a moment that he'd be expected to swig from one of the communal bottles. So he happily accepted his glass of Tricky Charms and discovered to his surprise that he quite liked it.

Of course, he ignored the tiny charm that

appeared on his glass. After all, he *was* a dragon. Too smart for trickery, even though the thought of adding the charm to his horde was rather tempting, especially since it was in the shape of a tiny flame. Still, he wasn't going to fall for temptation like the women did. He was actually feeling quite superior about it when he noticed his brother carefully extracting the charm from his own glass.

"Zee!" Markos exclaimed.

"For Ashlynn," Zee said as he shoved the charm into the pocket of his jeans.

Markos worried at first that something might happen, but as the hours passed and Zee's jeans didn't burst into flames (which honestly would have been quite hilarious considering Zee was a dragon wearing fireproof clothing), Markos decided he was just being paranoid. That didn't make him change his mind about his own charm, though.

Better safe than sorry, he figured.

As the hours passed, Markos decided that Charming was aptly named, for all the leprechauns had a fair bit of charm, not to mention they were entirely hilarious. They told endless jokes and ridiculous stories and generally kept everyone in their vicinity laughing all night long.

Laughing and drinking, that is.

In other words, they were all becoming increasingly drunk.

Tricky Charms turned out to be quite the potent drink and much to the dragons' chagrin, the leprechauns kept pace with their drinking all night long.

Kitty and Logan retired for the night several hours before closing, Logan leaving the dragons with one final admonishment. "Don't get too drunk and whatever you do, don't let the leprechauns take you with them."

Markos and Zee just laughed.

"Take us with them?" Markos exclaimed. "Isn't that what we want them to do?" He looked at Zee, who grinned drunkenly and shrugged.

Logan just shook his head and walked out with his arm slung around Kitty's shoulders, his head bent to murmur who-knew-what in her ear.

Markos figured it was probably sexy talk to get his mate in the mood or trash talk about the dragons' probability of success.

Possibly both.

That was okay though. The fairy would learn eventually that dragons never gave up.

Even when their mates demanded it.

Ashlynn had tried to convince Zee to leave when Logan and Kitty did, but he just dragged her into his lap and kissed her until she curled up quite happily and fell asleep in his arms.

Of course, she was supposed to be waitressing, but Cassie just grinned and announced that everyone would need to come to the bar for any future drinks.

Finally, last call arrived and it was time for the dragons to implement their plan.

Markos found himself a little conflicted, though, when it came time to actually follow the leprechauns. Usually he stuck around while Cassie closed down the bar, but that night, they had a mission. As the bar crowd began to thin out, he made a beeline for Cassie.

"You're going the wrong way, Markos." Zee hurried after him, dragging a sluggish Ashlynn in his wake. "The leprechauns are crazy fast. We don't have time for romance!"

"Hey!" Ashlynn exclaimed.

"It's true," Zee said. "Look around you."

Markos groaned. Zee was right. Half the leprechauns were already gone, even though Markos hadn't seen a single one actually leave.

At that moment, a commotion caught their attention, as Charming and a group of leprechauns snagged Princess Lucky from a table across the room, surrounded her and headed for the door, leaving Darren behind.

"Huh," Markos said. "Didn't know Darren was still here."

"Those are the last of the leprechauns," Zee hissed. "If we're going to follow them, we have to go now."

"Right," Markos said. "Hey, Darren, help Cassie shut down the bar, would you?" He then spun to face the door, staggering a bit as he did so.

Not because he was drunk or anything.

He'd just moved too fast, that was all. "Come on!"

Zee grinned. "Excellent."

"Love you, Cassie," Markos called over his shoulder, almost stumbling over his own feet in his haste to follow the leprechauns. "Back soon."

Cassie was busy counting money and just waved him on.

Markos stumbled out of the bar and screeched to a halt. Zee slammed into him from behind, then shoved him forward as Ashlynn slammed into both of them.

"Where'd they go?" Markos spun in a circle, stumbled into a wall, then righted himself.

The leprechauns had literally exited a split second before them and yet, the hall outside the bar was completely deserted. Not a single leprechaun in sight.

"I told you we didn't have time for romance," Zee growled.

"Whatever," Markos said. "I'm going to go help Cassie. We'll try again tomorrow." He headed back into the bar, fuming that the leprechauns had managed to escape him after all. Tricky bastards.

Darren couldn't help but snicker when Markos stormed back into the bar. Totally predictable.

"Back so soon?" Cassie asked with a big smile.

Markos let out a snarl that made Darren tense up, especially as the dragon stormed toward the bar, headed for his mate.

Darren got ready to intervene, but saw he didn't have to when Markos just kissed Cassie's cheek and muttered, "I'll catch 'em tomorrow."

These dragons were something all right. Stubborn, if nothing else.

With Darren and Markos helping (though
Markos was so drunk, he was more of a hindrance
than a help) they closed the bar fairly quickly and
headed out.

They were passing the lobby when Darren
caught sight of Lucky.

"You coming, Darren?" Cassie called from the
elevator. How she and Markos had managed to walk
right by where Lucky was perched without seeing
her, Darren had *no* idea.

"You guys go on ahead. I'll see you tomorrow," he
called.

Cassie called out something in reply as Markos
pulled her into the elevator, but Darren wasn't really
paying attention. He was too worried Lucky was
going to fall and kill herself.

What on earth was she doing?

He walked toward Lucky, incredulous at what he
was seeing.

Somehow Lucky had managed to stack two
tables upside down, one on top of the other. Even
more bizarrely, atop one of the legs of the second
table was a chair, also upside down.

And Lucky herself was standing on two of those

chair legs, delicately balanced, stretching toward a chandelier high above her.

Was she—she was! She was changing the light-bulbs in the chandelier. By standing on two upside down tables and a chair. It made no sense!

She was clearly insane.

The question was whether Darren could get her attention without causing her to fall.

He needed her down from there.

Right about that moment, Lucky noticed him for the first time.

They stared at each other for a long moment, Darren trying to ignore the fact that a single step forward would give him an exceptional view straight up her sassy, green skirt.

Finally, she said, "Darren?"

At that, he exploded. "What are you doing up there? Are you crazy?"

Lucky looked incredibly surprised, then shrugged, gave a tiny giggle and hopped down.

Literally.

She hopped from the chair's legs to one of the legs of the second upside down table, balancing there in what appeared to be a ballerina pose, one foot resting on the other. She made the landing without difficulty, but swayed in place, causing Darren to leap forward, arms stretched out as if to catch her.

"Aren't you sweet?" She winked at him, then leapt forward, landing in his arms, almost as if they'd planned it.

Stunned at his sudden armful of lush leprechaun, Darren stared into her eyes, then gently swung her legs down and set her on the ground.

Lucky smiled up at him. "I can't believe I messed up this trick!"

"What do you mean?" he asked.

"No one's supposed to catch us. That's the whole point. Yet here you are, staring right at me, catching me in your arms."

"You leapt at me like you *wanted* me to catch you."

"Well, who wouldn't? I mean, okay. Maybe a straight guy wouldn't, but otherwise, I'm pretty sure anyone would." She winked at him.

Darren was utterly speechless. He couldn't believe this gorgeous leprechaun was flirting with him. Sure, they'd flirted in the bar, but when her friends had swept her away at the end of the night, he'd figured that was that. A beautiful night, but it had ended with her walking away from him.

Yet, now, here she was, flirting again.

He was by far, the luckiest damn chameleon that had ever walked the earth. "You're enchanting." Wait. He hadn't meant to say that. But honestly, it was true, so why bother to deny it? "Utterly enchanting," he repeated.

Lucky blushed a little, peeked up at him from beneath her jaunty hat, then offered to walk him to his room. "But just a walk," she insisted, winking at him again.

Of course, Darren accepted, so off they went, Lucky skipping at his side, chatting a mile a minute.

As they walked, Darren began to notice the lights dimming as they passed them by, then brightening once they were past.

It wasn't until they reached his room that he realized all the light bulbs in the hallway were glowing green. "That's odd," he muttered.

Lucky looked around innocently. "What's odd?"

"The lightbulbs. They're all green."

"I like it," she said brightly.

Darren grinned. "Well, the lighting does complement your coloring very nicely."

She smiled. "You're so sweet, Darren." She hopped up and kissed him on his cheek. "I hope to see you tomorrow."

And then she disappeared.

Just like that.

One second there.

The next, poof.

She was gone.

                                    4

─────────────

*T*HE NEXT DAY when Darren ventured
downstairs, planning to meet his sister
and her mate for lunch, he found a rather hectic
scene in the hotel lobby. Guests were complaining
that their furniture had been turned upside down in
the middle of the night, *while they were sleeping.*

Harry, the hotel manager, looked overwhelmed
and Darren felt quite sorry for him.

"Darren!" Cassie hurried to him. "Can you
believe this?"

Considering what he'd seen the night before, yes.
He really could.

Interestingly, though, the lobby furniture
appeared to be in its proper place, no upside-down
tables in sight.

"The lobby looks fine," he said to Cassie.

"According to Lily, that's only because she and Harry spent an hour this morning setting it all to rights. When I saw her, she was cursing the leprechauns. Do you think they did this?"

"Probably." What he really meant was definitely, but he wasn't going to admit that he'd caught one of the leprechauns in action the night before. He wasn't sure if he was protecting Lucky or himself. Based on how aggravated Harry looked, he was thinking it was probably self-preservation.

"All the lights in my room are green!" An angry troll bellowed.

"Poor Harry," Cassie murmured. "Come on. Let's get out of here." She grabbed her brother's arm and led him outside to where Markos, Zee and Ashlynn were waiting.

"About time. I was afraid I was going to have to go in to save you from the masses," Markos said, pulling Cassie into his arms with a grin.

They spent the rest of the day in downtown Jamesville, having lunch out and wandering through the shops.

Well, the women shopped.

Darren and the dragons just stood around and chatted.

Eventually they ended up at a shop called The House of Light, where they met up with three witches and their shifter mates.

The women were apparently close friends, which is why Ashlynn and Cassie insisted the witches join them at the bar later that night.

"I thought we were going to Shenanigans 1 tonight and 2 tomorrow night," one of the cougar mates protested.

"Yeah," said the wolf. Karl, Darren thought his name was. "After we have dinner with your aunt Dory tomorrow."

"Well, I guess we're going to Shenanigans 2 two nights in a row," Megan said.

"Exactly," one of her sisters said, either Jessica or Lara, Darren wasn't sure.

"Just like we've been to Shenanigans 1 the last four nights in a row," the final sister said.

The rest of their day was uneventful, at least until they arrived at Shenanigans to set up the bar later that day.

All the tables were upside down, with bar stools on top of them, also upside down.

"Seriously?" Cassie did a fair imitation of a dragon's growl.

Markos chuckled. "Don't worry, darling. You go

get the bar ready. Darren and I'll deal with the furniture."

Darren couldn't even imagine the point of this. Was it just to be funny? Did leprechauns think turning people's beds upside down, while they were sleeping in them, was funny? Did they think it would be funny to eat and drink while perched on the leg of an upside down stool?

It was really quite the mystery.

They'd only managed to right about half the tables when patrons started arriving.

The leprechauns were first and they chortled and chuckled their way to the tables Markos and Darren had set back up, spreading out so that when non-leprechauns arrived, they either had to stand or help with righting the furniture they wanted to sit on.

Meanwhile, the leprechauns were drinking and laughing while watching patrons and employees bustle about, setting the bar to rights.

"You lot are a menace," Cassie called to them, which sent them into giggling fits. "I should cut you off."

This threat sobered the leprechauns immediately.

"You can't cut us off," Charming protested. "This is neutral territory."

Cassie scowled. "I have to let you in, but that

doesn't mean I have to keep Tricky Charms in stock. Or any alcohol for that matter. Maybe this will become a dry bar, did you ever think about that?"

This made the leprechauns fall all over each other, they laughed so hard.

"A dry bar! A *dry* bar, a dry *bar*, a *dry bar*," they chanted, giggling all the while.

Cassie just rolled her eyes, but Darren could tell she was charmed by the leprechauns' antics and wasn't really annoyed at all.

"So." Markos plopped into a seat at one of the leprechaun tables. "Let's drink!"

Unbelievable. The dragon wasn't giving up anytime soon.

Darren was about to join them when Lucky showed up.

He immediately abandoned the dragons in favor of spending the evening with his lady leprechaun.

As he walked away, Lucky on his arm, he heard one of the leprechauns say, "Haven't you heard, laddie? You've got to follow the rainbow if you want to find a pot of gold."

Cassie was hard at work, filling drink orders and wondering where Ashlynn was—the phoenix hadn't shown up for her shift yet—when Kitty arrived, absolutely filled with joy, dragging a disgruntled looking Logan behind her.

"Look, Cassie!" Kitty exclaimed, showing off her arms.

Cassie froze and leaned over the bar to stare. "Are those—"

"Tiny baby shamrocks! My freckles are turning Irish. Isn't that so cute?"

Before Cassie could really decide how she should respond to that question, Kitty exclaimed, "I have to go show the leprechauns. I'll be back!" And off she darted toward the leprechaun tables, Logan following in her wake, still looking rather put out.

If Cassie had to guess, she'd say the fairy wasn't too happy with the leprechaun magic that was clearly changing his mate's appearance.

At that moment, Ashlynn came sweeping into the bar, clearly in a rage. "Look at what those leprechauns did to me!"

Cassie's jaw dropped. She'd heard the phrase before, but this was really the only time it had ever happened to her. She couldn't even speak, she was so incredibly...

Dismayed?

Horrified?

She gulped.

Entertained.

Must not laugh. Must not laugh.

Now that Ashlynn was in front of her, Cassie realized she probably should have expected this result. After all, Ashlynn had a lot more freckles than Kitty and many of them were in tight clusters.

Still, she didn't think she could ever have predicted these results.

Though Cassie was looking closely, she couldn't really pick out any shamrocks. Well, maybe that giant cluster there. If she squinted her eyes and tilted her head just so, maybe that was a giant shamrock on Ashlynn's—

"My arms are completely green!" Ashlynn shrieked. "And my boobs—Ooooh, I'm so mad. They look like I've got patches of grass all over them. Or a disease. I look diseased, Cassie!"

Cassie was trying so hard not to laugh.

They were friends and Ashlynn was clearly upset, but this was just hilarious.

"What am I supposed to do?" Ashlynn wailed.

Cassie was pretty impressed she wasn't screaming at the leprechauns, who were really completely out of control at this point.

"Well, first, I'd suggest taking off the charm," Cassie said, raising her voice to be heard over the din of leprechaun giggles and, well, it had to be said, the guffaws of the dragons.

Ashlynn glared at Zee, who had followed her into the bar, a huge grin on his face, and who was now laughing with his brother. "I can't believe you find this funny!" She whirled back to Cassie. "And I can't get the necklace off. It's almost like it's been welded shut."

Cassie swallowed a giggle, cleared her throat and called across the bar again, "A total menace!"

This, of course, just set off the leprechauns again, some of them going so far as to fall to the floor where they rolled back and forth and laughed and laughed.

Cassie shook her head, hurried around the bar and gestured for Ashlynn to turn around.

Ashlynn swept her hair out of the way and Cassie tried to get the necklace unlatched.

"Damn," she muttered. "You're right. This is really hard to—I can't quite see where the latch is. It's like it's—I don't know."

"I told you! It's been welded shut!" Ashlynn wailed.

Thus began a round of all of the patrons (except the leprechauns) trying to get the necklace's latch to open.

The dragons tried melting the metal clasp.

The trolls tried brute strength.

The witches tried magic.

Nothing worked.

"Your friends are certainly having fun tonight," Darren observed.

Lucky giggled. "They're always happy when a trick comes out even better than planned."

"They didn't plan that?"

"Well, the thing about a good trick is that you *can't* plan it perfectly, no matter what you do because people are unpredictable. You have to send your trick out into the world and then wait for the results. Sometimes they're nowhere near as funny as expected and sometimes they're way funnier."

"Interesting." Especially because the theory

behind what she was saying very closely mirrored what they taught chameleons about their cons.

People were unpredictable.

Expect the unexpected.

"Take Kitty and Ashlynn, for example. It was the exact same trick, using the exact same charm, and yet the results were entirely different and their reactions were completely opposite from one another. There was no way for my frolic to know how either one of them would react, so they just set up the trick and waited for the results."

"Your frolic?"

"It's what we call a group of leprechauns. Family, friends, a clan, really."

"I like it. It's especially appropriate for your particular friends."

"Oh?"

"I mean, they're fun and irreverent and always laughing, so yeah. I bet it's a frolic a minute in your realm."

Lucky laughed. "Or at least a trick a minute."

5

____

ASHLYNN COULDN'T BELIEVE the trouble one small charm had caused and it was all for the enjoyment of those silly leprechauns.

She really wanted to be mad, but their general hilarity was so amusing, it was impossible not to want to laugh along with them.

She didn't, of course, because hello—green skin! Plus her mate was laughing enough for both of them.

When Kitty offered to ask Artemis for help, though, Ashlynn finally decided she'd had enough.

The fact that she actually considered saying yes to involving the goddess of the hunt meant that it was clearly past time to seek a solution from the source of the problem.

Ashlynn waved away the dragons and fairies and witches and trolls, not to mention the former handmaiden of a goddess, and headed for the table where the leprechauns had been thoroughly enjoying the show.

She settled in a chair and said, "This was quite the ingenious trick, but I'd really like to have my normal skin color back please."

"Ah, are you sure, lass? You look mighty pretty in that shade of green," one of the leprechauns said.

"I'm positive. Please?"

"All righty then." He reached out and touched a finger to the shamrock sitting in the hollow of her neck.

A slight tingle ran through her and she was utterly relieved to see the green appeared to be fading. Just a little.

"It'll take about twelve hours for the full effects to subside," the leprechaun told her.

"But they will go away?"

"They will."

"Thank you! What's your name again?"

"Jolly."

"Thank you so much, Jolly." Ashlynn leaned over and kissed his cheek, causing him to blush a brilliant red and Zee to roar in annoyance from where he was watching from across the room. "It really was a good trick." She stood and headed back toward the bar.

When Zee would have grabbed her as she walked by, she darted out of his reach and shook her finger at him. "Don't even think about it. I'm mad at you."

"Me? I'm not the one who turned your skin green!"

"No, you're just the one who laughed about it."

Zee scowled. "And who was that laughing like a loon last night?"

Ashlynn blushed. "Well, I'm sorry, but that was hilarious!"

"And this isn't? Personally, I think if anyone has the right to hold a grudge, it's me!"

"Hey, I deleted those photos." Something she'd regretted immediately after.

"Are you sure? Did you get every last one, even the ones in the cloud?"

Ashlynn bit her lip. "Maybe." Hopefully not though.

Zee growled.

"Hold on a minute," Markos interrupted. "I'm finding this conversation a little hard to follow. I got the whole Ashlynn's boobs are green bit, but I seem to be missing something. What photos are we talking about now? And are they recoverable because I sense an opportunity I would hate to miss."

Ashlynn giggled. "Well, see—"

Zee lunged for her and slapped a hand across her mouth. "Not a word, babe. Not one single word," he muttered in her ear.

Ashlynn giggled hysterically as he carried her out of the bar, Markos' voice following them into the hallway. "No problem, guys. I'll just bribe you later, Ashlynn!"

"What about your Coalition?" Lucky asked. "Is it a con a minute?"

Darren laughed. "Not even close. We could spend months setting up a con, years even if it's an especially complicated one."

"Really?" That seemed like it would require a lot of patience, something leprechauns weren't exactly known for.

"Definitely. Though we do always have different cons in motion. Some chameleons prefer to work alone, some in pairs, some in groups. The cons they choose reflect that."

"And you? Do you prefer to work alone or in a group?"

"I've always been really good at leading teams into some of our more complicated cons. Recently, though, I stepped into a leadership role, so now I'm responsible for helping the team leaders coordinate all the cons of the coalition, rather than leading my own."

"Wow." That sounded like a lot of responsibility, also something leprechauns weren't exactly known for. "Don't you get bored? Or impatient? Or bored?"

Darren laughed. "Sometimes. But I still love it and when I need a break, I take it. Like this week, hanging out with my sister, getting to know her mate, attending her mating celebration. Also, I do tend to jump into cons sometimes, you know, just to keep my skills up-to-date."

"And to escape the boredom, right?"

Darren laughed again. "Exactly right."

*T*he rest of the night was fairly uneventful to Cassie's way of thinking.

Zee and Ashlynn eventually returned and Zee joined his brother in their continuing quest to drink the leprechauns under the table.

"You'd think they'd have learned their lesson from last night," Ashlynn said. "Zee was a bear when he woke this morning."

Kitty giggled. "A bear-dragon."

"Exactly," Ashlynn said. "He was so hungover. He didn't appreciate it when I made him get up."

"Markos was annoyed as well," Cassie said. "Serves them both right."

"That's what I said."

Kitty giggled. "I thought Logan was going to insist on staying last night, but then he decided your mates were on their own."

"Smart fairy," Cassie said.

Kitty giggled. "I think it had more to do with the fact that fairies aren't that fond of leprechauns and vice versa."

"Really? But aren't leprechauns a type of fairy?"

"Yes, but they're trickster fairies, and I guess they have no problem playing tricks on their own kind, which the fairies don't appreciate."

She grabbed her drink and stood. "And on that note, I'm off to join my mate. See you guys later."

"Later," Cassie and Ashlynn chorused as Kitty walked away, headed for the table where Logan had joined the witches and their mates.

And so the hours passed, with the many paranormals in the bar drinking and laughing, and in the dragons' case, trying to get the leprechauns to reveal where their gold was hidden.

When Cassie announced last call, a flurry of orders came in as usual, then slowly, the bar began to empty out.

Surprisingly, the leprechauns weren't stealthily disappearing the way they had the night before.

"Great," Ashlynn said.

"What is it?" Cassie asked.

"They're just toying with them now. You know that, right?"

Cassie grinned. "Again, I feel very strongly that they'll be getting what they deserve."

"We're terrible," Ashlynn said. "We should be trying to protect our mates from the leprechauns' trickery."

Cassie stared at her incredulously.

Ashlynn burst into laughter. "I'm just kidding.

Zee freaking laughed at my green skin, although to be fair, I did laugh at his misfortune last night."

Cassie leaned forward. "Let me in on the secret? Please."

"Okay, but you can't tell Markos. He'd never let Zee live it down and Zee, well, he'd never forgive me for telling."

"My lips are sealed."

"Okay, so, basically, Zee had one of the charms in his jeans pocket. It was a tiny flame, so last night when he got undressed, well, let's just say certain things were fire-engine red, and as the night progressed, they got redder *and* hotter."

"You don't mean—"

"Yep. Zee kept sending me to the ice machine down the hall. He was *not* a happy camper."

Cassie snickered. "Well, at least it wasn't a shamrock charm."

"I think he might have actually preferred that. At least shamrocks aren't flaming hot."

They were both laughing when the lights went out in the bar.

A split second later, they came back, though darker—and greener—than before.

"Are you kidding me right now?" Markos bellowed from across the room.

Cassie glanced his way to see that he and Zee were sitting all alone at tables that only moments before had been filled with leprechauns.

"They did it again," Zee growled.

Ashlynn giggled and Cassie couldn't help but join her when Markos snarled, "Tricky bastards."

6

AS THE NIGHT progressed, Darren found Lucky to be increasingly charming and enchanting, and she seemed as interested as he was. He was gearing up to ask her out on a real date when suddenly the lights went out.

They came back on a split second later, but when they did, Lucky was gone.

All it took was a quick glance around the room to realize *all* the leprechauns were gone.

Darren sighed, then picked up his drink and joined the dragons at their now-deserted table.

"Not having much luck following the leprechauns, are you?"

"Oh, shut up," Markos growled.

"We'll figure it out," Zee said. "It can't be that difficult. We just need a plan."

Darren snorted. Like a plan was going to help these two. "You should leave it alone. The leprechauns are never going to let you get your hands on their gold, but you might just find your-selves without your hands if you're not careful."

"Don't be ridiculous," Zee said. "We're dragons!"

Darren shook his head, marveling at their stubbornness.

It didn't take too long to close down the bar and they all left together.

When they passed the lobby without a sign of Lucky, Darren was rather disappointed and entered the elevator feeling quite let down.

Cassie and Markos got off on the second floor while Ashlynn and Zee got off on the third.

Darren rode the elevator all the way to the fourth floor and had just turned the corner, heading toward his room, when he ran into Lucky.

She was standing in front of a portrait, appearing to examine it very closely.

"Now what are you up to?" Darren asked.

Lucky jumped and whirled around, looking startled.

And guilty.

Darren looked around, but he couldn't see anything amiss.

No stacked furniture.

No green light bulbs.

"Oh, hi, Darren." Cassie smiled at him innocently.

Yep.

She was definitely up to something.

"So what trickery are you up to tonight?"

"Oh, nothing. I was just out for a leisurely stroll." For a moment, she looked cross. "Though I can't understand how I'm getting worse at the tricks rather than better."

"Why do you think you're getting worse at them?"

"Because you keep catching me! You're not even supposed to be able to see me. Although I suppose it's only fair seeing as you're not exactly very good at the chameleon thing, are you?"

Darren jolted. "What do you mean?"

"Well, come on. Aren't I supposed to think you're a leprechaun or something?"

Darren hadn't really thought about it until that very moment, but of course, there'd be no reason for Lucky not to share what she was up to if she believed he was a leprechaun like her. Yet she hadn't invited him to join in the trickery. "Weird."

"I know, right? You can see me, even when I'm at my trickiest, and I know beyond a shadow of a doubt that you're a chameleon. Something's weird about this hotel I think."

"Or maybe—"

Before he could finish that thought, Lucky said cheerfully, "Well, gotta go. See you tomorrow, Darren!" She hopped up and kissed his cheek, then disappeared.

It was a repeat of the night before and it made him growl in frustration. "Great," he muttered. "Now I'm sounding like a dragon."

He'd been standing there for a full minute before he realized the painting Lucky had been examining now sported giant googly eyes springing from the bosom of the woman in the portrait.

The next several days were a pretty close repeat of the previous ones.

Cassie was getting nervous as her mating day approached and Markos wanted her distracted as much as possible so they went on several excursions. A day trip into the woods to visit the local wolf pack and another day spent wandering the fairy mall. Both days, Darren tried to focus on his sister and her mate to enjoy his time with them, but he was a bit distracted constantly thinking about Lucky and wondering what she was up to.

The evenings were spent at Shenanigans, flirting with Lucky and observing the leprechauns in all their goofiness, which ratcheted up every time a trick of theirs was revealed in all its glory.

A perfect example was when Kitty showed up thrilled with her bright green nails one night.

"I'm not sure about this, Kitty," Ashlynn said worriedly.

"Tell me about it," Logan grumbled. "You should see her when she shifts. She's green from the tip of her whiskers to the tip of her tail."

"Green whiskers?" Cassie asked.

"Green everything."

The leprechauns all giggled.

Logan glared at them while Kitty skipped over to them to show them her nails, all of which had tiny shamrocks in the center.

"Very pretty, lass." The leprechauns all complimented her on her green accessories and Kitty skipped back to Logan, looking incandescent with joy.

Darren shook his head.

Folly. This was utter folly.

More than his concern about Kitty's progressive greenery, though, Darren found Markos' obsession with finding the leprechaun's stash of gold utterly worrisome. Normally, he wouldn't care what a dragon was up to, but this was his sister's mate. He tried repeatedly to talk sense into the dragon, but every time he thought Markos might be about to come around, his brother Zee chimed in with another ridiculous idea.

When Darren wasn't trying to talk sense into the dragons, he was spending time with Lucky, flirting and falling in love.

Unfortunately, Markos and Zee eventually realized that Darren was seriously courting Lucky, and began to make a nuisance of themselves as a result, often joining them at the worst possible times.

Darren would send them pointed looks, but just like the stubborn dragons they were, they would simply settle in to torture him. Of course, invariably, much of Lucky's frolic would follow. And so Darren had not yet managed to ask her out on an official date.

It was almost as if Markos and Zee could predict the very moment Darren was about to bring up the subject for that was always when they descended upon them, leprechauns typically in tow.

With members of her frolic around her, Lucky was as sassy as ever. She would tease the dragons and the fairies when they joined them, riling both groups up as much as possible.

The dragons continued to try to trick the leprechauns into revealing the location of their gold while the fairies began a campaign to figure out a way to extend the banishment of the leprechauns from the mall to the bar and to the hotel itself.

It wasn't possible, of course, what with Shenanigans being neutral territory, but the fairies were certain there had to be a loophole somewhere and recruited the witches to help.

Unsurprisingly, the witches said the same thing, but with a lot of magical mumbo-jumbo to accompany it. The magic protecting neutral territory would always nullify any spells cast upon it. Nothing they could do magically. Blah-blah-blah.

And so the fairies pouted and the dragons fumed while Lucky and her leprechaun friends taunted and teased and laughed the nights away.

As expected, the dragons never managed to follow the leprechauns. "Tricky bastards," Markos would mutter each night when somehow they managed to disappear yet again from under their noses.

Darren was beginning to find it all terribly amusing.

Except for the part where they kept interfering with his attempts to court Lucky.

Happily, he still managed to catch her alone after leaving the bar each night.

One night, he followed the sound of tapping to find Lucky knocking a tiny hammer against a wall in the west wing of the hotel.

Innocently answering, "Nothing," when asked what she was up to, she accompanied him back to his room, holding his hand and chatting all the while. As they walked, she swung her free hand, the one holding the hammer, back and forth, tap-tap-tapping it against the walls.

That was the first night she gifted him with a kiss when they arrived back at his room. Well, she kissed him on his cheek every time she saw him, both coming and going, but this was their first real kiss.

One Darren hadn't even initiated.

Not that he minded. In fact, the minute she touched her lips to his, he was lost.

They dueled for control of the kiss, his tongue tangling with hers and vice versa, until they ran out of breath and would break for a moment, then one or the other would lunge forward and they'd be at it again.

Those long minutes spent in the hallway right outside his door, learning what made the other shiver in delight, were lost in a haze of passion, to the extent that Darren was always surprised to see how much time had passed when they finally parted and he staggered into his room, drunk on Lucky's kisses.

He'd almost forgotten about Lucky's tiny hammer until he left his room the next morning and saw shamrocks growing from the walls in great trailing vines.

He found Lucky's trickery to be enchanting, and even though he knew it wasn't hers specifically, he couldn't help but be amused at the charm trick that just kept growing and growing, as it did that very night.

"Oh my gosh, Kitty! Tell me you dyed your hair for St. Paddy's Day and that it's not a result of that stupid charm," Cassie asked.

"Nope. I just woke up to green hair."

Ashlynn shook her head. "Well, it may be gorgeous, but I wouldn't like not having control of my own body like that."

"You know," Darren interjected. "It might be a good idea to ask the leprechauns to turn off your charm before it gets really out of hand."

"Oh no," Kitty exclaimed. "I *like* it. I didn't even have to bleach my hair to get it this color. It's just naturally green."

Logan, on the other hand, didn't look quite as happy as Kitty. In fact, he spent most of the night glaring at the leprechauns. "This trick is getting out of hand."

"Oh, leave it be, Logan. I'm sure everything will be fine," Kitty said.

"You don't understand how tricky those leprechauns are. They can't be trusted."

"He's right," Darren said. "You never know what might happen next."

"I'm sure whatever it is will be simply wonderful," Kitty said.

Ashlynn snorted.

When the leprechauns disappeared literally into thin air—again—at the end of the evening, Markos was not happy.

Darren couldn't believe the dragons hadn't given up their quest yet. Talk about stubborn.

"How do they keep doing that?" Zee demanded.

Lily rolled her eyes. "You do realize leprechauns are fairies, right?"

"Yes, but they don't have wings," Markos protested. "How are they moving so quickly on those little legs?"

Lily giggled. "Not all fairies have wings, you know. And they're not a requirement for moving quickly. Leprechauns are trickster fairies. You can't trust them at all. And like all fairies, they can pop between the realms just like this." She snapped her fingers and with an almost audible pop, disappeared.

Harry growled. "I hate it when she does that. I never know if she's lurking or really gone."

"Lurking!" Lily reappeared from thin air. "How dare you? I'll show you lurking!" She reached out, grabbed the traveler by his lapels and this time, disappeared them both, all at once.

"This place is a nut house," Darren said to Cassie.

"I know. Isn't it great?" Without waiting for an answer, Cassie walked back to the bar, probably to begin closing it down.

"You know, I've been thinking," Zee said. "We've been trying to follow a bunch of leprechauns all at once. Maybe we should focus on just *one* instead."

"I like this idea," Markos said. "The question is, which one?"

They both turned and stared at Darren.

Darren narrowed his eyes at them. "Not a chance. I'm not joining your foolish games."

"But you've clearly managed to strike up a friendship with Lucky," Markos said.

"I bet she'd be happy to go for a walk with you. As soon as you get her outside, we'll grab her!" Zee said.

Darren scowled. "You two need to stay away from my Lucky."

"*Your* Lucky?" Markos grinned.

"So it's like that, eh?" Zee slapped Darren on the back. "Good for you, man. Having a mate is the most amazing thing."

Darren froze. He hadn't really considered that Lucky might be his mate. He'd had the thought briefly a couple nights before, but then it had evaporated in a haze of passion.

It made sense though.

Except for the part where she was from an entirely different realm. That didn't make a whole lot of sense. Why would he be matched to someone he might never meet?

Then again, his sister's mate was from a different realm.

In fact, it seemed a bit of an epidemic around

Shenanigans.

Mates from different realms finding each other at the bar.

Perhaps they were being drawn together by forces none of them expected.

The dragons were still chatting and laughing, but Darren was distracted thinking about all the possibilities.

Suddenly, he felt extremely motivated to get on with his night. He hurried over to his sister. "Hey, Cassie. You need my help closing down?"

"Nah. You go on. I'll see you tomorrow for lunch, yeah?"

"Yeah." Darren leaned across the bar, kissed her cheek, gave the dragons a nod, then headed out.

As he walked to the elevator, he practiced what he was going to say.

First, he'd mention the possibility of them being mates, then—no, wait. That might make it sound like he only wanted to date her because they might be mates.

Okay.

First, he would ask her out on a date, then if the date went well, he'd bring up the possibility of them being mates.

Yes.

This was a good plan.

Now if only the elevator would arrive.

He was contemplating taking the stairs when the doors finally opened to reveal Lucky leaning against the back wall, eating marshmallows.

Darren stepped inside the elevator and raised an eyebrow at her.

"What are you up to now?"

"Nothing," Lucky said innocently (the same thing she said every night), then offered him a marshmallow.

Darren accepted it, but didn't take a bite. Instead, he could only stare as Lucky slowly devoured her own marshmallow, licking her lips and tempting him greatly.

When she was finished eating, she reached for his hand, the one holding the marshmallow he had yet to eat, and lifted it to her lips.

He gently fed the marshmallow to her, breath hitching when her lips closed around his fingers and licked them clean.

The elevator arrived and they slowly exited, lost in a haze of attraction.

They walked slowly to his room, eating marshmallows along the way, feeding them to each other and stealing long, drugging kisses.

When they finally reached his door, Lucky said, "Will you meet me for lunch tomorrow? Maybe around two?"

Even though he had just confirmed lunch with his sister, Darren didn't even hesitate. "Absolutely. Where?"

"How about in the lobby? We can have lunch in my realm."

Darren grinned. "I'd love that."

"Awesome! It's a date then." And with a quick hop and a kiss, she was gone.

It didn't even occur to Darren until he was relaxing in bed that he'd never actually managed to ask her out on a date. Instead, she'd asked him.

He fell asleep with a smile on his face.

7

HE NEXT DAY, Darren met his sister in the lobby around noon as they'd already planned, but after explaining his lunch plans with Lucky, swore her to secrecy.

"What's the big deal?" Cassie asked.

Darren just raised an eyebrow, which made her giggle.

"Okay, fine. I guess it's probably a good idea if Markos doesn't realize you're hanging out with a leprechaun this afternoon."

"Where is Markos anyway?"

"He's so hungover, I couldn't get him out of bed this morning."

Darren grinned. "Okay, color me not surprised at

all. Those leprechauns have been getting the dragons drunk night after night."

"I know!" Cassie exclaimed. "You know what the most hilarious part about that is?"

"That the dragons believe *they're* the ones getting the *leprechauns* drunk?"

"Exactly!"

As Darren laughed with his sister, he was so incredibly grateful he'd decided to come out a full ten days early, just to see her. He'd missed her and it was so nice being able to laugh with her and get to know her mate.

Even better, he was starting to think the dragons were right, and he'd gained something even more valuable than time with his sister this trip.

"So, is she really your mate?" Cassie asked.

She must have been reading his mind. "Markos told you, huh?"

"Yep."

"I'm not sure. Maybe. Probably."

"What makes you think so?"

"In addition to the incredible chemistry?"

"Ew, I don't want to hear about that!"

Darren laughed. "She knew I was a chameleon right from the start, never once thought I was a leprechaun. Plus I keep catching her playing tricks in the hotel."

"You've been catching her? She hasn't been hiding while doing them?"

"She seems to think she's hiding, which could mean—"

"That you're seeing through the veil to your true mate!"

"Exactly."

"Darren, I'm so happy for you!" Cassie flung herself into his arms and hugged him tight.

"Yeah, well. There are a lot of unknowns. I mean, I'm head of the Coalition. She lives in a whole different realm and is a leprechaun princess."

Cassie waved a hand in dismissal. "Lucky told me the title's a relic of the past. They don't really have royalty anymore."

"I know. But still. Am I really going to take her away from her people?"

"Darren. She's a leprechaun. They're fairies. She can pop between the realms on a whim. And she can probably take you with her. Lily's always dragging Harry along when she pops in and out of the realms."

"Huh. I never even thought of that."

"I say go for it. You like her, right?"

Darren grinned at the memory of the mischievous look on Lucky's face as she switched out the lightbulbs while balanced on the leg of a chair, and of the innocent smile she greeted him with right after attaching googly eyes to a painting, and of walking hand in hand with her while feeding each other marshmallows. "I think I love her."

"Oh, Darren. That's just so lovely."

Darren was thinking about how happy Cassie was for him a couple hours later when he met up with Lucky in the lobby of the hotel.

One moment he was standing on his own, the next the elevator doors opened and an adorable leprechaun popped her head out and waved him to her. "Darren!"

He smiled and jogged to the elevator, backing her into it and stealing a quick kiss. "Where to, sweet Lucky?"

She spun to face the elevator buttons and pushed the 2nd and 3rd floor buttons at the same time.

The doors closed, the elevator gave a small lurch, then slowly climbed from the first floor to the second, and began to inch its way to the third. It stopped right in between the two floors and the doors opened to reveal a giant field of clover.

As they exited the elevator, Darren exclaimed,

"How exactly did that happen?" He turned to stare at the elevator and watched as it winked out of existence. "The other day, Cassie pushed the same two floors, but we ended up in the fairy mall."

Lucky laughed. "Oh, Darren. You should know the answer to that question."

"I should?"

"Of course. The elevator's in a Hotel Shenanigans and *that's* how that happened."

That non-answer hurt Darren's brain, though from all the stories Cassie had told, it was clear Hotel Shenanigans was a rather spooky place.

"Right. Well. As long as we can get back." He paused. "We *can* get back, right?"

Lucky giggled. "Of course we can. Come on!" She grabbed his hand and led him deeper into the field until they reached the edge of a light green blanket spread across the clover.

The blanket had a dark green shamrock in the center and each corner was pinned down by shamrock-shaped stones.

Off to the side of the blanket was a huge picnic basket.

"Wow, Lucky. This is amazing."

Lucky beamed at him. "I hope you're hungry."

"Famished."

Lunch was delicious and they talked for hours, about everything and nothing, pausing every once in a while to punctuate their conversation with long kisses as they rolled across the blanket and fed their passion.

Eventually, they wore each other out and fell asleep in each other's arms, Lucky's head pillowed on Darren's chest.

He played with her hair until he eventually fell asleep and it was the most restful sleep of his life.

When he woke, Lucky was sitting at his side, smiling at him.

He leaned up on his elbows and she leaned down to kiss him.

"You know what?" she whispered against his lips.

"What?"

She lifted up to stare in his eyes. "I think we might be mates."

Darren surged up and swept her into his lap. He kissed her, pouring all of his joy at finding his mate into the kiss.

When they finally pulled away, he said, "You know what?"

"What?"

"I do believe you're right, sweet mate of mine."

Lucky squealed in joy and hugged him tight, then kissed him again.

As the day's light started to wane, they packed up the picnic supplies and trash, folded the blanket and began to walk, hand-in-hand, back toward where the elevator had dropped them off.

"It's my lucky day," Darren said.

"It is?" Lucky asked.

"I found my mate and look!" He leaned over and plucked a clover from the ground. "I also found a four-leaf clover."

Lucky giggled.

He handed the four-leaf clover to her, then leaned over and picked another one. "Hey. Are they *all* four-leaf clovers?"

"Maybe." She gave him a sassy smile and tucked into her hair the clover he'd handed her so that it sat at a jaunty angle over her ear. "Well, I suppose I should get going. My frolic will be wondering where I am."

"More tricks to play, I take it?"

She shrugged. "Maybe."

At that moment, the elevator reappeared right in front of them.

"How does it do that?" Darren demanded.

Lucky shrugged. "I told you. It's a Shenanigans

elevator." She pulled him in behind her and pushed the lobby button.

They kissed all the way back to the earth realm.

When the elevator doors began to open, she pulled away and said, "I'll see you tonight," and then she was gone.

That night at Shenanigans was about as predictable as it could be, Darren thought.

It all began with Kitty's arrival.

"Look, my eyelashes and eyebrows turned green! They match my hair and my eyes now. I mean, my eyes have always been green, but now it's like my whole body is an accessory for my eyes!"

"Um, I'm not sure this is a good thing, Kitty," Cassie said.

"Why not? It's just a bit of fun."

"Well, do you want to stay green for the rest of your life?" Ashlynn asked.

"Who said anything about the rest of my life? I'm sure it'll wear off eventually. In the meantime, I'm going to enjoy it!"

"I just don't understand it!" A commotion at the door had everyone looking that way. Megan, Jessica and Lara were storming into the bar, accompanied by their mates.

"All of Dory's plants are blooming marshmallows," Megan exclaimed. "What's up with that?"

"I kind of like it," Karl said.

"You would!" Lara scowled. "How many of those things did you eat anyway?"

Karl grinned. "Not enough. We should stop at your aunt's on the way home for another snack."

"How can we cast spells with our herbs if they're all sticky and marshmallowy?" Jessica demanded.

The leprechauns all started giggling again.

"Marshmallows are yummy," Mischief exclaimed.

"Tasty," Bossy agreed.

"Someone did you a tricky favor," Joker said.

"They're right," Charming said. "You should be grateful."

The witches just glared at them and grumbled some more before eventually deciding they needed to buy more herbs and stormed out again.

*L*ucky was sitting at a table, flirting with Darren, when the dragons finally stumbled in. They looked somewhat ragged, what with the bloodshot eyes and hair standing on end.

Darren shook his head. "I think maybe your frolic should give the dragons a break tonight. Don't you think?"

Lucky grinned. "Oh, come on. When your cons are going well, do you just give them up?"

Darren scowled. "I suppose not. So tell me about your favorite trick."

Over the next several hours, Lucky shared the stories of her favorite tricks and listened to the stories of Darren's favorite cons.

The more they talked, the more Lucky realized he was quite the trickster himself.

As she listened to his story of the con in Ireland where her brethren bested his, she couldn't help but grin as he explained how some poor chameleon named Jackson managed to get stuck in a fairy mound.

"We had to pull him out. It really wasn't easy and well, his leg got a little mangled in the process."

Lucky hated to giggle at someone's misfortune,

but really, they deserved it. Targeting a family protected by leprechauns was quite the misstep. When she pointed that out, Darren just nodded.

"True that. We haven't stepped foot in Ireland since."

"Probably a good idea. Do you like leading your Coalition?"

"It's a pretty good deal. We have a lot of fun. You should join us on a con sometime. Between we chameleons and you leprechauns, the cons we could manage would be glorious."

Lucky loved that idea. "Oh, and just imagine the mischief we could cause!"

They grinned at each other.

"Is Zee feeling as horrid as Markos?" Cassie asked Ashlynn.

Ashlynn giggled. "Oh, I'm not sure there's a being anywhere who feels worse than Zee right now. I told him he shouldn't come out tonight. Seriously, I'm starting to worry about alcohol poisoning."

Cassie laughed. "Okay, I shouldn't laugh, but they're dragons. Can you imagine the amount of alcohol they'd have to consume to poison themselves?"

"Well, I'm pretty sure they've made a good start."

The women stared at where Zee and Markos were once more hanging out with the leprechauns and like the idiots they were, desperately attempting to get them to share their secrets.

Of course, they were doing this by drinking heavily.

Again.

Cassie shook her head. "I doubt they'll make it the night."

Ashlynn grinned. "Agreed. Unconsciousness has to be imminent."

Cassie laughed.

As it turned out, Ashlynn was right.

The night wasn't half done before the constant overindulging finally caught up with the dragons.

Too much alcohol combined with not enough sleep night after night meant one minute they were laughing uproariously and the next they were both passed out under the tables while the leprechauns giggled and drank toasts to the foolish dragons.

Ashlynn and Cassie did their duty, of course, by taking a plethora of pictures and immediately texting them to everyone they knew.

Then Cassie went a step further and posted them to the Shenanigans boards, the comments on which entertained both women for the rest of their shifts and made it worth having to shut down the bar without the assistance of their mates.

For once, the leprechauns managed to slip away without causing the dragons endless frustration, if only because they were still unconscious.

8

———

HE NEXT DAY, Cassie and Ashlynn were quite entertained by their extremely grumpy dragon mates.

Uncertain whether to blame the leprechauns or the women more, both Zee and Markos spent the day glaring and grumbling.

They'd woken on the floor of the bar, under a couple tables, covered in crumbled nachos, bits of pretzels, peanut shells and popcorn kernels.

Crawling out from under there at close to ten in the morning, they were extremely disgruntled to realize they'd been abandoned by their mates, and they made this known to both Ashlynn and Cassie all day long.

They were still grumbling when they arrived to open the bar later that evening.

"You should look at this as a sign," Cassie told them.

"Exactly," Ashlynn said. "You do know stealing is wrong, right?"

"Please," Zee said. "It's not exactly stealing if they can't protect what's theirs."

"Yes, it is," Ashlynn said. "It's totally stealing."

"Yeah, that's the very definition of stealing," Cassie agreed.

"Eh. Maybe by earth standards," Markos said. "But I'm pretty sure their pots of gold aren't on earth."

"Exactly," Zee said. "It's just that following the leprechauns to their realm has been a bit trickier than we expected."

"Right," Ashlynn said, drawling the word out. "Because if you managed to somehow make it to the leprechaun realm, I'm sure they'd be just fine with you stealing their gold and wouldn't do anything to keep you from leaving with it."

"Eh, we're dragons," Markos said. "What could they possibly do?"

"Dragons," Darren groaned as he walked up to join the conversation. "So arrogant."

"Hey. That's what makes us so good at what we do," Markos said. "You do know that all we really need is to catch one."

"Exactly," Zee said. "If we manage that, we can demand to know where their gold is and they'll have to tell us."

"Plus we know someone who can catch one for us." Markos grinned at Darren, who scowled back at him.

"I already told you no."

"Leave Darren alone," Cassie said. "Besides, if that's all there is to it, then why haven't you caught one yet?"

"Yeah," Ashlynn said. "You've been drinking with them every night."

Zee looked horrified. "Shenanigans is neutral territory. We can't just snatch a leprechaun from the bar."

"Or the hotel," Markos said.

"And that's why we have to follow them *out* of the hotel," Zee said. "Then we can grab them and make them take us to their gold."

"I had no idea you were so morally bankrupt," Ashlynn said to her mate.

"Hey, all's fair in hoarding and war," Zee protested.

"Exactly," Markos said. "Why do you think dragons have hordes? Because we're the best hoarders in all the realms."

"And the best thieves," Zee said.

"Beg to differ," Darren said.

"Oh no," Cassie said. "Do *not* encourage them."

"What? I'm just saying. No one is better than a coalition of chameleons."

Cassie snorted. "Unless you're going up against a frolic of leprechauns."

"Come on, Zee. We're not going to get any sympathy here." The two dragons wandered off.

Darren winked at his sister, then followed them to a table full of leprechauns.

No Lucky yet, Cassie saw, but she figured it wouldn't be long.

Kitty wandered up to the bar at that moment, looking rather glum.

Cassie examined her closely, but couldn't see any new green on her, which could be good if it meant the charm's magic was finally wearing off or it could be very bad if its effects were now being felt where they weren't easily seen.

"What's the matter, Kitty?" Ashlynn asked.

Kitty gave a big dramatic sigh. "I don't think anything turned green today."

Cassie bit her lip to keep from laughing.

Because Kitty was very wrong.

Cassie glanced at Ashlynn who gave her wide eyes in return.

"So, Kitty," Cassie said. "Did you happen to brush your teeth this morning?"

"Gross. Of course I did."

"And you didn't notice anything new?"

"Nooo. Logan was still sleeping when I got up so I brushed in the dark." Her eyes widened. "Are my teeth green?"

"Here." Ashlynn pulled a compact mirror out of her purse and passed it to Kitty.

Kitty took one look and let out a shriek of horror. "My tongue is green! It looks like a slab of moldy meat!"

"Well. At least it's not your teeth," Cassie said.

"Not yet anyway." Ashlynn smirked.

Kitty stared in the mirror. "I'm really not liking this development." Her eyes narrowed. "And I do *not* believe that Logan didn't notice. He's kissed me like a thousand times already today." Her eyes widened. "This is why everyone at the hotel was looking at me so strangely! I bet they thought I did it on purpose!"

She whirled around and yelled at Logan across the room, who was keeping his distance, for obvious reasons. "You're in so much trouble! No more kisses for you!"

Logan grinned. It was obvious he knew he had nothing to fear in that regard.

"Dang it." Kitty swung back around to face the bar. "He's so sexy, I'll never be able to follow through on that one."

"And why would you want to?" Ashlynn asked, making Kitty giggle.

"Okay. I don't. But still. He should have told me!"

"Agreed," Cassie said. "But you know, I think maybe you should consider asking the leprechauns to put an end to their tricky charm."

Kitty sighed. "I suppose. But I really liked the green hair and the nails and even the tiny shamrocks."

"Fear not," Ashlynn said. "We can totally get all of that done at the fairy mall. The fairies are quite talented with nails and hair and I bet we could even get them to apply some temporary tattoos for you."

"Or even a real one," Cassie said. "I hear the trolls have a tattoo parlor in the mall."

"Oooh, good idea." Kitty hopped off the stool. "Well, I'm off to throw myself upon the mercy of the leprechauns. Wish me luck."

As Kitty walked off, Cassie said to Ashlynn, "My plan worked."

"What plan?"

"Look." Cassie nodded toward the leprechaun table, where Lucky was now sitting in Darren's lap.

"Oh my goodness!"

"I know. Val really came through for me. He looks so happy."

"This deserves a toast!" Ashlynn said.

"Incognito?"

"Dragon flame."

"Gotcha."

Cassie pulled out two bottles, one of Incognito for her and one of Dragon Flame for Ashlynn. She poured out their shots and stared in amazement as the alcohol turned green the minute it landed inside the glass.

"That's weird," Ashlynn said.

"I know." Cassie picked up her glass, but nothing happened.

No change of colors, no mixing rainbow.

"Hey! Where did all my colors go?" She glared across the room at the leprechauns, who apparently always knew when one of their tricks was about to come to fruition because they were all staring at her, huge grins on their faces.

"Aw, it's just a wee bit of green," Topsy called out.

"A wee bit? It should be a rainbow of colors!" Cassie exclaimed.

"Eh. Green is so much better, don't you think?" Impy asked.

"But I thought you guys liked rainbows," Cassie protested.

The leprechauns all glanced at each other, then chorused, "Propaganda."

"Wait a minute. Does that mean your pots of gold *aren't* under a rainbow after all?" Markos demanded.

Charming grinned. "That's for we leprechauns to know and you dragons to never find out."

The dragons growled in frustration.

Cassie sniffed at her glass. "Well, still smells like Incognito." She clinked her glass against Ashlynn's. "To Darren and Lucky."

"To true mates."

They bolted back their shots and grinned at each other.

"This is ridiculous!" The doors burst open and Megan, Jessica and Lara trooped inside, their mates directly behind them.

"What now?" Cassie asked when they reached the bar.

"All the water in Dory's room has turned green!" Lara exclaimed.

"Really?"

"Yes! And none of our spells are turning it back." Megan scowled.

"Even the toilet bowl water's green," Jessica said.

Her words set off the leprechauns who started up a storm of chortling and giggling and laughing.

"That's a good trick," Silly said between laughs.

"Who thought that one up?" Caper asked.

"Me." Tricky sent a mischievous grin their way. "I thought it'd be funny to pee in green water."

If the leprechauns thought green toilet bowl water was funny before, the thought of actually peeing in said water was so hilarious they almost fell to floor, they laughed so hard.

"This is getting out of hand," Markos said.

That's when the fairies arrived.

$\mathcal{D}$ARREN WAS ENJOYING playing with Lucky's hair when Lily stormed into the bar, clearly furious, with a number of unknown fairies at her back.

"Uh-oh," Logan said.

"What is it?" Kitty asked.

"Looks like Lily ran out of patience. Those are all very high-ranking fairies from our realm."

"This is completely out of hand," Lily raged at the leprechauns. "There are green shamrocks all over the floors, googly eyes and shamrocks on the walls, our reservation computer has turned into a giant shamrock, all the hotel rooms and the keys for those rooms are no longer labeled with numbers, but instead with shamrocks. *Shamrocks!*" She shrieked.

"Everywhere I go, it's shamrocks, shamrocks, shamrocks.

"How am I supposed to know what key to give our guests, not to mention how are they supposed to find their rooms if they're all labeled with shamrocks?" She paced back and forth in front of the giggling leprechauns, flinging her arms this way and that, wings fluttering in fury.

"Every single floor is labeled with arrows indicating this way for these numbers or that way for those numbers, but guess what those signs say now? Shamrock to shamrock this way!" She flung one arm to the left. "Shamrock to shamrock that way!" She flung her other arm in the opposite direction.

She whirled to face the leprechauns who were clearly having the time of their lives, chortling and chuckling as the fairy ranted and raged at them. "How are we supposed to have a functioning hotel if you leprechauns keep messing things up?"

Silence.

"Well?" Lily shrieked.

"Were you wanting an answer?" Charming asked.

"Of course I want an answer," she shouted.

"I just want to be clear," Charming said, a ridiculously innocent look on his face. "Are you accusing the Leprechaun Nation of being responsible for these terrible occurrences?"

"Terrible occurrences? You mean tricks, don't you? Tricks you people specialize in!"

"Oh, now, that's harsh," Lucky said.

Darren had a hard time containing his chuckle and he knew Lucky could feel his chest shaking in amusement.

"It really is," Charming agreed.

This was just getting better and better. The sibling leprechauns were hilarious when they got going.

"After all," Lucky said. "We're just sitting here, innocently minding our own business, having a wee drink with friends." She glanced over her shoulder at Darren. "And mates." She gave him a quick kiss, then turned back to the fairies. "Then, out of nowhere, we're suddenly being accused of *terrible* misdeeds."

"Oh, go sell that troll manure somewhere else!" Lily snapped, making Darren snort with laughter. He'd never seen the fairy quite so riled up before. "Just tell us! What exactly do you want?"

Lucky shook her head. "I don't understand."

"Nor I," Charming agreed. "Whatever gave you the idea we want something?"

"Because leprechauns are never *this* annoying!

You want something and I know it. So just tell us what it is and maybe we can negotiate."

At that word, Markos and Zee appeared to perk up.

"Fine," Lucky said. "We'd like our banishment lifted."

"Seriously?" Lily exclaimed. "You cause all this mischief and think it will convince us to *lift* your banishment?"

"Hold on a minute. What banishment?" Markos asked.

"The fairies banned the leprechauns from ever setting foot in the fairy realm, which just so happens to include the fairy mall, a good three hundred years ago."

"Why would you banish paying customers?" Zee exclaimed.

"Because they never paid," Lily snarled.

"What are you talking about?" Charming protested. "We always paid."

"Yes, with your magic coins," Logan said.

"Magic coins that are no good in here, by the way," Cassie called from the bar.

The leprechauns all gasped.

"Cassie, we would never try to use our magic coins in neutral territory," Lucky said. "Why, that might actually get us banned from all Shenanigans everywhere!"

"Like you were banned from the fairy mall?" Lily asked.

"Oh, come on. That was just a few bad actors and you banished our entire species! Plus we're fairies like you," Lucky said.

"She's right," Charming said. "I honestly can't believe you would banish your own kind like that."

"But you're not like us," Lily exclaimed. "You're tricky, tricky fairies and we don't like being tricked.
"

"Well, that's not very kind of you, judging us just because we like a good trick now and then," Mischief said.

"Yes, and let's be clear," Lucky said. "Our banishment had nothing to do with our magic coins. It was that ill-fated love affair."

"Ugh. Not that stupid story again," Logan groaned.

"Those two *were* stupid," Lily agreed.

"What are you talking about?" Zee asked.

"Well," Lucky began. "Legend has it that once upon a time a fairy princess fell in love with a leprechaun prince."

Darren grinned. Lucky had told him this story

just the night before. He was interested to see if the fairies agreed with the leprechauns' version of it.

"The only problem was," Charming said, "their parents hated each other with a passion."

"Something about a trick one leprechaun played on a fairy about a hundred years before these two were even born," Lucky said.

"Seriously?" Zee exclaimed.

"Oh, yes," Logan said. "Fairies can hold quite the grudge."

"And it was a horrible trick," Lily exclaimed.

"It was brilliant!" Charming protested.

"*Anyway*," Lucky said. "These two fell in love, but their parents were determined they would *not* spend their lives together."

"Even though legend has it they were mates," Charming said.

"So, the fairy family, desperate to end the match, got all the fairies riled up about magic coins in the mall and got the leprechauns banished. This meant, of course, that the leprechaun could no longer venture into the fairy realm to visit his lover. This didn't stop the fairy from visiting him, of course. Unfortunately, the leprechaun prince blamed the fairy princess and her family for his people's banishment and they had a terrible fight. She ran away in tears and got caught in a storm. He caught up with her just in time for the two of them to be swept away in a flood."

"Of course, both families blamed the other," Charming said, "and there was no forgiveness to be found. The banishment became permanent and leprechauns have not been welcome in the fairy realm ever since."

"That's a terrible story," Ashlynn exclaimed.

"I know!" Lucky said. "Can you imagine? Never being able to shop at the fairy mall? Now *that* was a cruel and unusual punishment."

"I was talking about the prince and princess."

"Oh, yes. That was sad too."

"But not as sad as our banishment," Charming said.

"Especially since we weren't even using those magic coins on the fairies," Lucky said. "They punished us when we weren't even targeting them."

"Oh please, you know that fairies don't run every shop in the mall," Lily said. "Management was getting constant complaints from the trolls, the dragons, the gryphons, the gargoyles, the mermaids, the—"

"Yes, yes, we get it," Charming said. "But they didn't even try to negotiate."

"Negotiate?" Markos leaned forward. "We dragons love to negotiate."

"No, no." Lily said. "There will be no negotiating with leprechauns. They cannot be trusted."

"How rude!" Lucky exclaimed. "I cannot believe you would tarnish every leprechaun with the same brush."

"Disappointing," Charming agreed, "and such a shame the fairies are so bigoted."

Lily gasped. "We're not bigoted!"

"Really?" Lucky asked. "Because I'll have you know that leprechauns are very trustworthy. You can trust us to keep our word."

"And strictly your word," Logan said.

Lucky grinned. "Exactly."

"Look. We can't help you with your banishment from the fairy realm," Markos said. "That's up to the fancy-schmancy fairies to decide. But we *can* help you with the fairy mall."

The leprechauns all smiled.

"We know," they chorused.

"Wait! You can't do that," Lily exclaimed.

"I don't understand," Ashlynn said. "How are you going to help them again?"

"Well, the fairy mall may be *called* the fairy mall,

but about half of it happens to cross over into the dragon realm," Markos said.

"And that half," Zee said, "belongs to the dragons."

Darren grinned. Suddenly all the leprechaun tricks in the hotel and at the bar were making a whole lot more sense.

"So," Markos said to the leprechauns, "What are you offering?"

"Commerce, of course," Lucky said. "We leprechauns love to shop, so you can pretty much be guaranteed a lot of sales if we're given access to the dragon side of the mall." She glared at Lily and the fairies standing behind her. "Though the fairies certainly won't benefit."

"Also," Charming said, "Shoes."

"Shoes?"

"Yes. We would like a store in the mall to sell our most excellent shoes. It would be a boon for all the beings of the realms, to have access to the leprechauns' greatest inventions."

"Are they as awesome as our fairy slippers?" Ashlynn asked.

Charming frowned. "Fairy slippers?"

Lily spun and frantically shook her head at Ashlynn, who look confused.

"What's this about fairy slippers?" Lucky asked.

"Oh, nothing, I'm sure," Lily said.

Lucky narrowed her eyes, leaned forward and glared at Lily. "She wouldn't happen to be talking about our very popular, very expensive *leprechaun* slippers, now would she?"

"Oh, where would you get that idea?" Lily looked rather nervous.

And guilty.

Darren feared quite suddenly that these negotiations might end in war.

And all because of something called fairy slippers, or leprechaun slippers, as the case might be.

"She is!" Mischief leapt to his feet. "How did an earth being get her hands on our slippers?"

Everyone stared at Ashlynn, who said in a hesitant voice, "I bought them at the mall?"

"The fairy mall?" A roar echoed through the room as the leprechauns, though full of mischief usually, proved they were also most definitely fairy when they got mad.

"Our slippers are being sold in a mall we've been banished from?" Charming snarled.

"And you're calling them fairy slippers?" Lucky screeched.

Darren thought she might have leapt across the

table and strangled Lily if it weren't for the fact that he had an arm around her waist and was busy stroking a soothing hand down her back.

"Okay. Let's all calm down," Zee said. "It's clear there's been a bit of confusion around these slippers so perhaps we should open negotiations with that issue. Here's the thing. Lily doesn't own the mall or sell the slippers. So, we need to get the right fairies to the table."

Lily looked over her shoulder at the five fairies who had followed her in, but up to that point had remained silent.

The one at the center nodded and stepped forward. "*We* are the right fairies." With that pronouncement, all moved forward to sit across the table from the leprechauns, and negotiations began in earnest.

It took hours, even with the dragons acting as mediators.

Darren was quite impressed.

He would never have thought the dragons had it in them for such diplomacy, but they were truly skilled at working through the centuries of bad blood and anger on both sides.

The fairies eventually admitted they had spies who would slip into the leprechaun realm and purchase leprechaun slippers that they then turned around and sold at the fairy mall at a very high upcharge.

Darren worried that Lucky might explode, she was fairly vibrating in rage at that point, but she managed to contain her fury and channeled it into negotiating furiously for a percentage of the profits from the last three hundred years.

The fairies protested this might bankrupt them, but apparently they were quite rich, something that seemed to be public knowledge, so no one really believed them. As a result, the fairies eventually conceded, though they negotiated fiercely for as small a percentage as possible.

The leprechauns were also granted a shop inside the mall on the dragon side, of which the dragons would reap a percentage of sales.

At this point, the fairies demanded to know where the benefit was for them.

"You've given them everything they wanted and we've gained nothing," Lily protested.

Markos just raised an eyebrow. "You banished them for centuries, yet still profited off their ingenuity. And you call *them* the tricksters? Perhaps you should be grateful we've managed to broker peace and try negotiating some good will to go with it."

"Well," Lucky said. "If you lift the banishment from the *fairy* side of the mall, the fairies might enjoy quite a bit of profits from leprechaun commerce."

"Likewise," Charming said, "if you lift the ban from the fairy hotel, you might find a lot of leprechauns are spending their hard-earned money to stay there."

The fairy who had taken the lead in all the negotiations glared at the leprechauns, then said, "Only if the leprechauns agree to *never* use their magic coins on *any* fairy property *ever again.*"

"Agreed!" Every leprechaun in the room chorused in unison and negotiations were finally concluded.

Lucky rewarded Darren with a passionate kiss, and the celebration, both in the bar and later in Darren's hotel room, lasted all night long.

10

IT WAS FINALLY time for Cassie's mating ceremony, which was taking place at Starlight, a night club in the fairy mall.

This meant that since the leprechauns' banishment had been lifted, they expected an invite as well.

As a result, her ceremony wasn't quite as elegant as Ashlynn and Zee's had been.

Instead, it was raucous and loud and full of hilarity and mischief.

Every drink served was green and shamrocks were everywhere, but Cassie didn't mind. She spent the evening dancing with her mate, mostly lost in a haze of joy and lust, though Darren did steal her away for a brother-sister dance.

"Are you happy?" he asked her.

"So happy. All my dreams have come true. How about you and Lucky?"

He grinned. "She's met the members of the Coalition who are here for your ceremony and she's planning to go back with me when everyone leaves tomorrow. We'll figure it out. A bit of time in her realm, a bit in ours, a lot of cons, a lot of tricks."

Cassie grinned up at him. "It's going to be a beautiful life, Darren."

"It really is."

"I'll claim my mate back now." Markos executed some complicated dance move, somehow pulling Cassie into his arms while passing Lucky, with whom he'd been dancing, into Darren's.

The last Cassie saw of her brother, he was swaying in place, staring into his mate's eyes, clearly enchanted by what he saw there.

"I love you, Lucky mine."

Lucky's heart clenched at those words. "I love you too, Darren. I can't believe how lucky we are. We found each other, even though we were living in different realms."

"And I can't imagine a more perfect mate–match," Darren said. "The trickster and the conman."

"It sounds like some cheesy romance novel."

Darren grinned. "Well, we are experiencing our own happily ever after."

"We are."

They dance for hours, only breaking apart once more, this time to allow Lucky a dance with her brother.

"Only one," she warned.

Charming grinned and swung her out across the dance floor, then pulled her back in. "We did it, Lucky."

"I know. I can't believe it."

"The greatest trick our Nation has ever attempted and we made it happen."

"Was it really a trick though? I mean, we got what we wanted, sure, but in the end, they agreed."

Charming laughed. "Of course, they did, darling. Those fairies weren't going to risk the sheer volume of trickery the entire Nation was willing to bring their way."

"You don't think they might have just abandoned the hotel? I mean, it's happened before."

"Not a chance. Did you see that fairy with her

mate? That hotel is his legacy. She would never make him give it up."

Lucky smiled. "You're right. So we won."

"We did."

Kitty danced in Logan's arms for hours on end. She loved the feel of his arms around her and the way he slid his fingers through her hair.

She especially loved how he liked to play with the one green streak that hadn't yet faded.

"Dance, my lady?" Jolly approached with a grin on his face.

Logan scowled, but Kitty just patted his hand and murmured, "Let it be, Logan." She stepped away from her mate into the leprechaun's arms. "So what kind of mischief have you caused this evening?"

"Me? Cause mischief? I don't know what would give you that idea."

"So you're not responsible for the toilet bowl water that's green or the fact that the wedding cake has shamrocks for a bride and groom or the green strobe lights or—"

"Oh no, not at all. This is Cassie's mating celebration. We would never play tricks, though we might leave her a few gifts."

"Ohhh. Gifts, are they?"

"Indeed. You know that earth saying, 'Something old, something new, something borrowed, something blue?'"

"Yes."

"Well we decided it should be 'Something lucky, something mean, something Irish, something green.'"

"Oh dear."

When Darren finally managed to reclaim Lucky from her brother, he told her, "You're mine for the rest of the night. No more dances with anyone else but me."

Lucky smiled and stepped into his arms. "That sounds perfectly lovely."

And so they danced the night away in each other's arms, enveloped in a cocoon of love and joy and wonder.

"Oh no," Megan groaned.

"What is it?" Jessica asked.

"What are *they* doing here?"

"Who?" Lara asked.

"The Covingtons."

"No!" Jessica exclaimed. "Where?"

"There." Megan nodded across the room and her sisters swung around to stare.

Their twin cousins stood across the room, almost identical in appearance, but so very opposite in personality.

"They're friends of Cassie," their aunt Dory explained. "The three of them worked together at a Shenanigans a number of years ago and have kept in touch ever since. I'm going to go say hello."

Lara waited until Dory was out of earshot before she spoke again. "This place is doomed."

"We should evacuate," Jessica said, "and not just the club. The entire mall."

Megan burst into laughter. "Oh come on. They're not that bad!"

"Their out-of-control casting almost burned down their high school," Jessica said.

"Not to mention when they turned their cat blue," Lara exclaimed.

"And that car accident on highway nine," Jessica said. "It's a miracle no one was hurt."

"Also, that mini hurricane. If you hadn't been there, Megan, to spin it out to sea, I have no idea what would have happened," Lara said.

"They were young then," Megan said. "Surely they have better control by now."

"Control? You have met Serena, haven't you? I mean, look at her. Here a few minutes and already surrounded by leprechauns. That is not a good combination," Lara said.

"Not at all," Jessica said. "So I repeat, we should definitely evacuate."

Megan sighed. "Well, at least Samantha has some control."

The three of them switched their attention to Serena's twin, who was standing at rigid attention, listening and nodding solemnly to something a leprechaun was saying to her.

The leprechaun was giggling and gesturing, but Samantha wasn't even smiling.

"Too much control, if you ask me," Lara muttered.

Megan groaned. "And here I was hoping she'd

have learned to loosen up, even if just a little, by now. That control combined with her sister's lack of it—" She shook her head.

"Terrifying," the three sisters said in unison.

Read on to meet the Covington twins in an excerpt from *No Rest for the Wicked.*

There was something about Jack cuddling sweet Lexi in his arms and looking so natural doing it, that made Samantha's heart rate pick up.

Handing the little girl off to her older brother, Jack turned to Samantha and winked.

A wave of heat rushed down her spine and she spun on her heels, intending to hurry away.

Except somehow her body overrode her mind and she swung back around, grabbed him by the hand and dragged him out of the main room and down the hall to the walk-in linen closet.

She jerked open the door and pushed him inside, followed him in and closed the door behind her. All the while, her brain was shrieking, "Abort, abort!"

Hands on hips, she advanced on him. "What exactly are you doing?"

Jack looked a bit stunned. He glanced around at the shelves of towels and cleaning supplies, then back at Samantha. "Uh. I think that should be my question. What are *you* doing, Samantha? Not that I mind being dragged into a linen closet." He waggled his brows at her.

Samantha's heart gave a little leap and then began to race. Damn the man. He was messing with her equilibrium and taking total advantage. "My mother put you up to this, didn't she?"

Jack looked confused. "What are you talking about?"

"Oh stop acting so innocent. You're taking advantage of the reckless curse."

"The reckless—"

"You need to stop being—" She waved her arms in the air.

"Being what?"

"So very much you!"

Jack grinned at her.

That freaking sexy grin again. She just couldn't take it.

"And who exactly am I supposed to be if not me?"

Samantha growled low in her throat, then lunged at him.

She caught him by the lapels, dragged him down and kissed him.

Heat spiraled through her and then Jack took over the kiss.

He backed her against the door, leaned into her and utterly ravaged her mouth.

Only the door and his hands on her hips kept her from sinking to the floor in a puddle of goo.

Long, wicked moments later, he pulled away from her mouth to trail a line of kisses across her check and down her neck, then back up again.

"Damn," he muttered in her ear, bringing her back to her senses.

She pushed against his chest, trying to get a bit of space between them, trying desperately to catch her breath and to think for a moment. Dear goddess, everything was spiraling out of control, most especially her own emotions and actions. What had she been thinking, dragging this utterly scrumptious man into a linen closet with her? She was supposed to be avoiding him, not attacking him.

"I have to go." She pushed him back and reached for the doorknob behind her. "I have to get back out there, but—" She caught a breath at the thought of everyone seeing her in this state of agitation. "Do I look okay?" She reached up and patted at her hair, then smoothed down her shirt. She looked down at herself, but couldn't tell if she was put together enough to fool the press and anyone else who saw her.

And what if someone saw her exiting the closet? What if someone had seen her dragging Jack *into* it? This was a nightmare.

Jack chuckled. "You look beautiful, as always." He reached out a hand and tucked a lock behind her ear.

Samantha's breath hitched in her throat as she stared up at him. God. He was just so— "No. This, this right here is what I'm talking about." She waved an arm through the space between them. "You need to stop it. Stop acting so damn sexy." And she stormed out of the closet.

It wasn't until she'd reached the main room that she realized she hadn't even looked first to be sure no one was in the hall to see her exiting the linen closet.

She was utterly doomed.

*J*ack stared at the linen closet door as it slammed behind Samantha's retreating form, then grinned.

"Damn."

He just hadn't seen that coming at all.

But now that he had Samantha's taste on his tongue and seared into his memory banks, now that he'd experienced her passion, there was nothing that would keep him from claiming her as his own.

He was fully invested now.

Samantha Covington's days as a single witch were numbered.

Start reading No Rest for the Wicked *today.*

Please consider leaving a review on

your favorite book site.

If you would like to be notified of

Pepper's new releases, please sign up here:

www.peppermcgraw.com/newsletter

Undercover Shenanigans

Spooky Shenanigans

Holiday Shenanigans

Valentine Shenanigans

Lucky Shenanigans

STORIES OF THE VEIL

Guardians of the Veil

Astra

Glory

Luna

Zara

WICKED

No Rest for the Wicked

Wicked Is As Wicked Does

ANTHOLOGIES & COLLECTIONS

PAWSITIVELY PURRFECT BUNDLES

THE CAT'S MEOW

A Pawsitively Purrfect Trilogy

SHENANIGANS SERIES

CRAZED

Books 1-3

AMAZED

Books 4-6

HOLIDAZED

Books 7-10

SHENANIGANS

The Complete Collection

WICKED DUET

WICKED

ABOUT THE AUTHOR

WWW.PEPPERMCGRAW.COM

PEPPER MCGRAW is a *USA Today* Bestselling Author of paranormal romance. She hasn't met any paranormals to date, but she's sure that moment is just around the corner!

Pepper loves animals, especially cats, and spends her free time volunteering at local shelters and for Trap-Neuter-Release programs.

She's had the supreme honor of winning occasional head butts and meows from the local ferals in her neighborhood and has even convinced a few to come inside and adopt her as their own.

BB bookbub.com/authors/pepper-mcgraw

f facebook.com/peppermcgraw.author

g goodreads.com/peppermcgraw

instagram.com/peppermcgraw_author

tiktok.com/@peppermcgraw

twitter.com/peppermcgraw

www.ingramcontent.com/pod-product-compliance
Lightning Source LLC
Chambersburg PA
CBHW040536170726
48295CB00012B/494